Special lo
my great
great grandson
GramB

To our children, Ed, Susi, Margo, and Capt. Tom, and all sock monkey doll lovers. I want to thank the many people I have met. Thank you to old friends and new that made my old age so much fun, and for supporting so many happy sock monkey doll happenings!

– Barbara Gerry

Illustrated by Angie Scordato

Edited by Angela Malavolti

Published by Jungle Wagon Press

Rockford, IL

Library of Congress Control Number:2013958058

ISBN: 978-0-9834092-9-8

Printed in Rockford, IL

Mookie and I live with Captain Tom in a small blue house in the city of Rockford, Illinois. The Rock River flows through our back yard.

We sit on a velvety blue sofa that once belonged to the captain's grandmother. There are two large blue cushions–one on each end of the sofa. Mookie is curled up asleep on his pillow. I am perched up against the other. Mookie likes to nap. Several times a day he will hop up next to his cushion. His droopy eyes will close and very quickly he will be asleep.

I can still remember the magical moment when I came to life, when Captain Tom's mother gave me a beautiful face with a big red smile and stuffed me with love. She completed her masterpiece by sewing on a tail, two ears, arms, and a big red heart for all to see. She bounced me up and down on her knee. Up, down, up, down. She threw her head back and laughed with glee. For she had just finished a most wondrous creation. Me!

I peered up again at my maker and smiled as only a monkey doll knows how. Her eyes sparkled as she spoke to me, "You know that every monkey doll is different, unique? You are a work of art, really!" Then she laughed again, "Aren't you the wild one? Oh, the love you will bring! I will name you Rocky, for Rockford is the town of your birth. In the early days, a shallow, rocky ford was the only path across the Rock River."

In that moment I felt a heart throb. I knew I had a purpose. To love. To love like Captain Tom's mother loved me. I could feel every inch of stuffing within me tingle with her love. And I was meant to share it.

She gave me to Tom when he was just a boy. Now he is a grown man with a grown dog, Mookie. He is brown with long floppy ears, and a tail that is always wagging, especially when Captain Tom arrives home. He hears the car door slam and the Captain whistle as he comes up the steps to the front door. Mookie jumps off the couch and is at the door to greet him, jumping up and down he is so happy to see his master.

"Come on Mookie," the Captain calls, "Time to go for your run. I've got your leash." Mookie, his tail wagging happily, follows him out the door. The Captain climbs on his bike and off they go down to the park and to the corner cafe for their supper. Mookie just loves that. But I am left alone. Like every other day I sit quietly at my end of the sofa. I am tired of being here in the same spot night and day. After a while I hear them come home, slowly climb the steps and very sleepily head off to bed.

Soon they fall asleep. I know because I can hear them snoring. I am going to try to get off of this sofa. I begin to test what I can do. First I move my head from side to side, then my arms, and tail. I roll over onto my stomach and ease myself down over the sofa's edge and fall to the floor. I cannot believe that I am actually doing this! I pull myself upright and start to walk. Every step I take amazes me! The bedroom door is partially open, and I peek around it.

The bed is beautiful. I am going to get in it! I can climb just like all monkeys can. I pull myself up the post and slide down under the covers. I fall fast asleep with my wiggly eyes open wide.

Mookie wakes up. “Bark! Bark! Bark! Bark!” He is startled to see my head on the pillow! Captain Tom wakes and sits up rubbing his eyes. “Why are you barking so, Mookie? I was having a very happy dream.” Mookie keeps barking and nuzzles me with his nose. “Now Mookie, this is my special monkey doll. You mustn’t remove him again from his special place on the couch. Go back to sleep, Mookie, we’ve got a boat ride tomorrow!” With that I am placed right back where I started.

It is finally morning! Mookie is waiting for Captain Tom. I slide off of the blue sofa, scramble down to the kitchen and hide under the table. I want to know what breakfast is all about. Neither the Captain nor Mookie notice me hiding here. It's easy for me to be quiet; being a stuffed doll made from an old pair of socks, I can't make any noise!

FLOUR

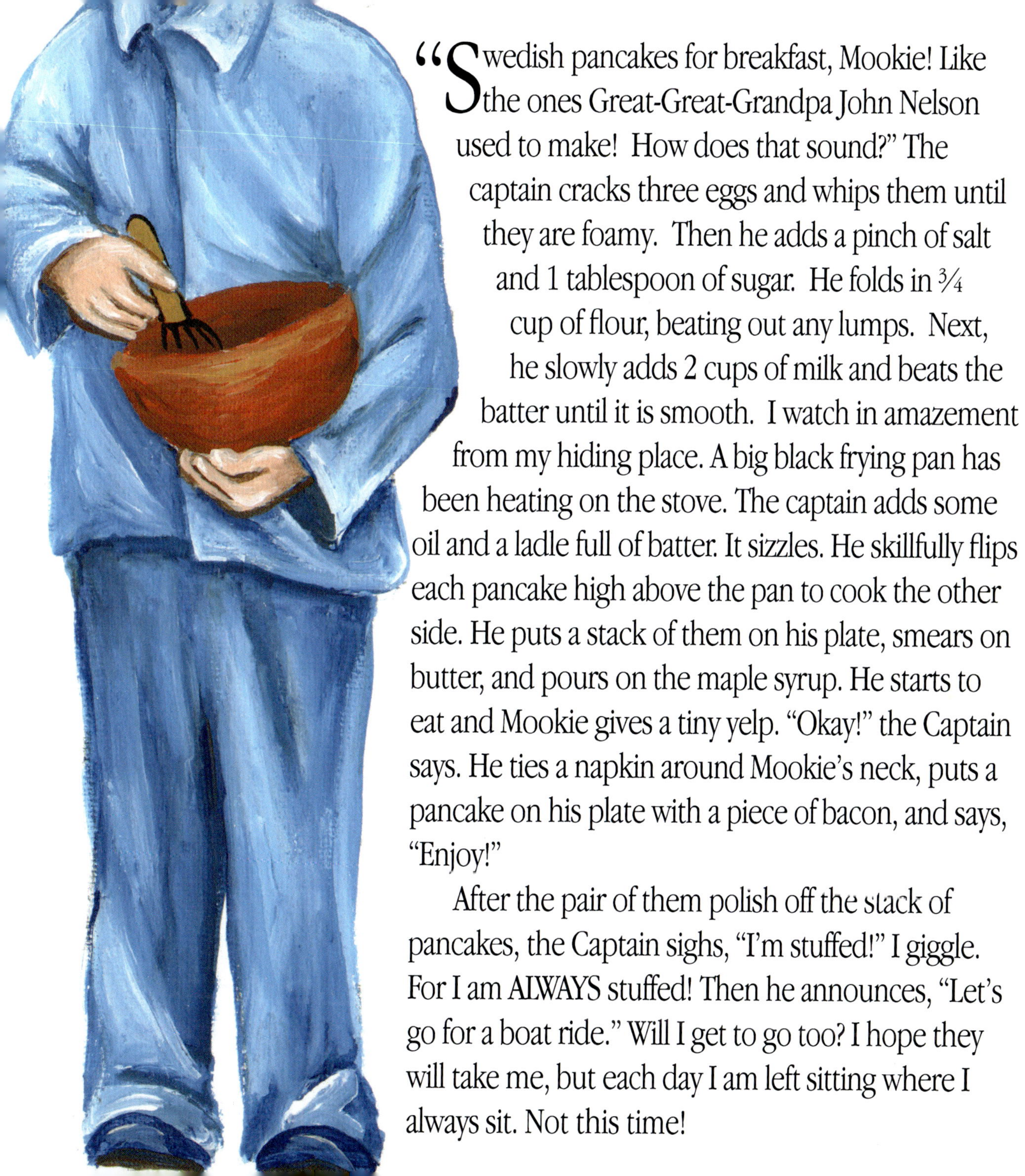

"Swedish pancakes for breakfast, Mookie! Like the ones Great-Great-Grandpa John Nelson used to make! How does that sound?" The captain cracks three eggs and whips them until they are foamy. Then he adds a pinch of salt and 1 tablespoon of sugar. He folds in ¾ cup of flour, beating out any lumps. Next, he slowly adds 2 cups of milk and beats the batter until it is smooth. I watch in amazement from my hiding place. A big black frying pan has been heating on the stove. The captain adds some oil and a ladle full of batter. It sizzles. He skillfully flips each pancake high above the pan to cook the other side. He puts a stack of them on his plate, smears on butter, and pours on the maple syrup. He starts to eat and Mookie gives a tiny yelp. "Okay!" the Captain says. He ties a napkin around Mookie's neck, puts a pancake on his plate with a piece of bacon, and says, "Enjoy!"

After the pair of them polish off the stack of pancakes, the Captain sighs, "I'm stuffed!" I giggle. For I am ALWAYS stuffed! Then he announces, "Let's go for a boat ride." Will I get to go too? I hope they will take me, but each day I am left sitting where I always sit. Not this time!

I am determined to go. Captain Tom rummages around in the closet and comes out with two life preservers. Mookie's is a small children's size. The Coast Guard says that everyone who goes out in a boat has to have a preserver on. They are bright orange so you can be easily seen in the water. While the Captain is putting his on, I slide off the couch, run to the closet, pull out a preserver, run back, and sit in my corner again. Mookie is the first to notice the life preserver next to me. He hops on the sofa and wags his tail. "Bark! Bark! Bark!" The Captain spins around, throws up his hands and exclaims, "I give up, Mookie! You can bring Rocky along for the boat ride." I feel honored as the Captain himself snaps me into a life vest!

Safely aboard *The Vindicator,* we ease out onto the Rock River for a fun ride! All kinds of boats were about: float boats, speed boats like ours, some boats even pulling children on water skis as they skimmed across the waves from side to side.

We pass a large building with real dinosaur skeletons on display! We see an outdoor playground a monkey could spend hours swinging in!

We pass under some bridges and Captain Tom comes along side of a dock and ties off the boat. He strolls inside a small restaurant for a sandwich leaving Mookie and me in the boat. Lots of people stop by to see us and Mookie barks at each one and I smile my big red smile and wiggle my eyes, flirting with them.
This is a happy and new experience.

Soon Captain Tom returns to the boat. He releases the lines and hops safely aboard. We are heading back home! What a wonderful day it has been! What adventures will tomorrow bring?

The History of the Rockford Sock Monkey

1852 — John Nelson, Swedish inventor, sailed to the U.S. with the first group of Swedes.Their destination was Chicago but a cholera epidemic caused a turn in fate. They traveled on and settled in Rockford, Illinois.

1879 — John Nelson was granted a patent for his sock knitting machine.

1880 — Nelson Knitting Company was incorporated, thus beginning the manufacturing of socks. Theirs was the first seamless heal and toe sock. It was comfortable and very inexpensive and worn by farmers and factory workers. If one pair wore out, they distributed three pairs for free!

1883 — John Nelson dies of pneumonia.

1891 — John Nelson's sons formed the Forest City Knitting Company.

1914 — American soldiers fighting in World War I wore Rockford socks.

1929 — Although no one knows when the first monkey was made from a pair of socks, it is told that during the Great Depression, many women took to sewing monkey dolls from old work socks. The monkeys were given as gifts to children who didn't have much else to play with.

1932 — Howard Monk, a wise advertising executive, suggested that Nelson Knitting add the red heel to distinguish their ORIGINAL socks from all the rest! The red heeled socks became a favorite for monkey-making since the red heels made such great monkey smiles!

American soldiers fighting in World War II wore Rockford socks.

1942-1945

1954

Forest City Knitting merged with Nelson Knitting.

Fox River Mills of Iowa bought the rights to the red heeled sock and continues to manufacture them. They aren't exactly the same, however. All socks are currently made on circular needles, and all have seams in the toe.

1992

2005

In an effort to celebrate and reconnect the city of Rockford with its own history, Barbara Gerry, great-granddaughter of John Nelson, in conjunction with the Midway Village Museum, opened a sock monkey exhibit at the museum and commissioned the creation of several fiberglass sock monkey dolls and the popular seven-foot monkey doll. "Nelson" was sewn with 42 pairs of socks!

The Midway Village Museum of Rockford, IL hosted its first "Sock Monkey Madness Festival." It has become an iconic, annual gathering place for sock monkey fans worldwide!

2004-2005

2008

Eighteen fiberglass dolls were placed on display throughout the city of Rockford.

Barbara Gerry authored and published *Rockford Sock Monkey Tales*, sharing her family history and love of sock monkey dolls with generations to come!

2014

About the Author

When Barbara Gerry's great-grandfather, John Nelson patented the seamless sock knitting machinein 1880, little did anyone know the long-lasting and far-reaching impact his invention would have. The warm sturdy socks made at Nelson Knitting factory were worn by soldiers, farmers and laborers. After John Nelson's death in 1883, his sons left Nelson Knitting and formed Forest City Knitting in 1891. His son, William, was president of both companies. After William, Barbara's grandfather Frithiof Nelson became president followed by her father, Edward Eisner.

One of Barbara's favorite memories as a child was spending time at the Forest City Knitting factory. She and her siblings didn't have baby sitters and were left in the care of their grandfather and dad at the factory if Mother needed to go somewhere. They got to know everyone, those in the office as well as the knitters. They loved watching the socks being made. There were big bins on wheels and they pushed each other around the floor in them! The company was family oriented.

In 1990, Barbara and her husband Elbridge, returned to Rockford to care for her parents after raising their children in Texas. In 2002, Barbara came to Midway Village Museum and reminded everyone of the history of the sock knitting machine and sock monkey. She suggested we share this piece of Rockford's history with the community. And then the fun began! Barbara's creative vision, indomitable spirit and positive attitude rebirthed the lovable sock monkey. Barbara and Elbridge funded Midway Village's Sock Monkey Exhibit, the fiberglass sock monkey display, and the creation of Nelson, Rockford's beloved seven foot sock monkey made from 42 red heeled socks!

The search began for former employees of the Nelson Knitting Factory. A community celebration was held and factory workers were interviewed. Their stories became part of the monkey exhibit at Midway Village. Nelson started traveling: from New York television appearances to Disney World, and even the Grand Canyon, his touring reminded the world that Rockford is where it all began!

In 2005, The Midway Village hosted its first Sock Monkey Festival. Sock monkey aficionados came from across the country and the world – an artist from California, a photographer from New York, and authors from as far away as Japan. The Sock Monkey Festival continues each year in March with activities for all ages. Families create sock monkeys together; they enter sock monkeys in the Ms. Sockford Pageant; a myriad of vendors arrive with unique sock monkeys and accessories.

Noteworthy too is the list of famous people for whom Barbara has made sock monkeys: President Barak Obama, Senator Dick Durbin, Congressmen Don Manzullo, Rob Simmons, Princess Estelle Sylvia Ewa Marie, future Queen of Sweden!

Due to Barbara's insight and tenacity, the museum received state and national recognition for sharing this rich history and engaging the community. In addition, the sock monkey dolls have been an economic engine for local, national and worldwide commerce…to say nothing of the joy and luck the precious little dolls continue to bring to children of all ages around the world. -Joan Sage